The Three Little Pigs

illustrated by Sally Anne Lambert

Ladybird

Once upon a time, there were three little pigs.

One day, they went out to build their own houses.

The first little pig built his house of straw.

The second little pig built his house of sticks.

The third little pig built his house of bricks.

Along came a big,
bad wolf. He went up
to the house of straw.

"Little pig, little pig, let
me come in," said the
big, bad wolf.

But the first little
pig said, "By the hair
of my chinny, chin, chin,
I will not let you in!"

"Then I'll huff and I'll puff and I'll blow your house down," said the big, bad wolf.

And he huffed and he puffed and he blew the house down!

The big, bad wolf went
up to the house of sticks.

"Little pig, little pig, let
me come in," he said.

But the second little
pig said, "By the hair
of my chinny, chin, chin,
I will not let you in!"

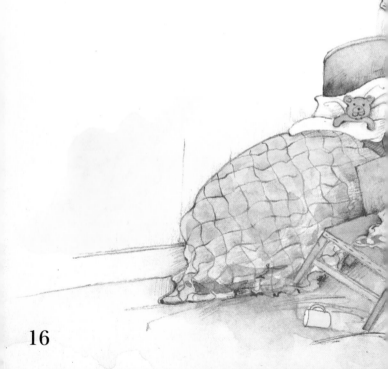

"Then I'll huff and I'll puff and I'll blow your house down," said the big, bad wolf.

And he huffed and he puffed and he blew the house down!

The big, bad wolf went
up to the house of bricks.

"Little pig, little pig, let
me come in," he said.

21

But the third little
pig said, "By the hair
of my chinny, chin, chin,
I will not let you in!"

"Then I'll huff and I'll
puff and I'll blow your
house down," said the
big, bad wolf.

So he huffed and he puffed and he huffed and he puffed, but he could not blow the house down.

The big, bad wolf climbed on top of the house and came down the chimney…

25

Splash!

And that was the end of the big, bad wolf.

26

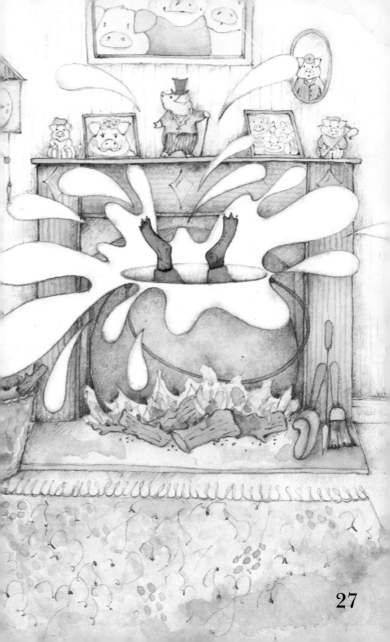

27

Read It Yourself is a series of graded readers designed to give young children a confident and successful start to reading.

Level 2 is for children who are familiar with some simple words and can read short sentences. Each story in this level contains frequently repeated phrases which help children to read more fluently. Every page in the story is accompanied by a detailed illustration of the main action, which aids understanding of the text and encourages interest and enjoyment.

About this book

The story is told in a way which uses regular repetition of the main words and phrases. This enables children to recognise the words more and more easily as they progress through the book. An adult can help them to do this by pointing at the first letter of each word, and sometimes making the sound that the letter makes. Children will probably need less help as the story progresses.

Beginner readers need plenty of help and encouragement.